# *PROLOGUE*

It is said that long ago gods and goddesses ruled over the earth, sky and seas. Terrible monsters threatened those who dared to cross their paths; oracles warned of the future in prophecies; and bold heroes performed brave deeds. Among the most courageous of these heroes was Perseus, who came to be known as "The Gorgon-Slayer". This is his story.

# *THE PROPHECY*

**In an ancient city stood a tall tower, plated in brass. It reflected the sun in a dazzle that could be seen from far away. Imprisoned within the tower was a beautiful princess, Danae, the only daughter of King Acrisius.**

A terrible prophecy had foretold that Danae's son would kill his grandfather.

"I will never let her give birth to my grandson," Acrisius declared. "If I lock Danae away from other people, she will never fall in love, so the prophecy can never come true!"

So Danae lived alone. No one saw her except an old servant-woman, and King Acrisius, who visited once a year. The people of the kingdom walked past the tower and wondered what secrets it held.

"Maybe it's full of treasure!"

"Maybe it's the home of a powerful goddess!" they guessed.

One day the great god, Zeus, was intrigued by the shining tower. Looking through the walls he saw the beautiful Danae.

Changing himself into a shimmering mist, Zeus entered the tower by a high window. He and the delighted Danae spent many happy days together.

"Please don't leave me alone," Danae begged him, when Zeus had to leave. "I am so lonely here."

Zeus had grown to love Danae so he granted her wish. In time she gave birth to a son, whom she named Perseus. She loved him dearly.

## *BANISHED*

Before Acrisius made his yearly visit, Danae hid the sleeping baby in a wooden chest. When the bolt on the door was thrown back and the king strode in, he looked at her suspiciously.

"Have you spoken to anyone?" he asked.

"Whom could I speak to? How could anyone enter this strong tower?" she answered cleverly. Acrisius was satisfied, but as he turned to leave, Perseus, woken by the strange new voice, gurgled loudly.

Acrisius turned white with rage. Flinging open the chest, he looked down at the smiling baby. This was the grandson he had dreaded.

"How dare you disobey me," he yelled. "I banish you from my kingdom for ever!"

Danae and baby Perseus were locked in the wooden chest and cast out into the raging sea. Danae clutched Perseus tightly trying to protect him as the roaring waters battered the chest.

Hours passed as they were swept along, until, suddenly, Danae felt a heavy thud. Then all was quiet.

## *DICTYS*

On the shore of the island of Seriphos, a fisherman, called Dictys, was drawing in his nets from the water.

"The sea is rough tonight," he thought. The nets were heavy as he hauled his catch onto the beach. Suddenly, they seemed tangled, so he waded into the shallows. There, amidst the flapping fish, was a battered wooden chest.

"What treasure have I dragged up from the deep?" he wondered. Using a piece of driftwood, Dictys levered open the lid. To his amazement, he found a beautiful woman, cradling a baby in her arms.

# *THE CHALLENGE*

Perseus and Danae lived on Seriphos with Dictys for many years. As Perseus grew up he spent his time fishing or listening to his mother's stories of their past.

"Your father is a powerful god."

"Am I a god too?" he asked.

"No, but you are a prince," she said. "Your grandfather, Acrisius, is a great king."

Perseus became very proud and boastful, often challenging his friends to duels with wooden swords.

Polydectes, the king of Seriphos, was a cruel tyrant. All the nobles in the kingdom, including Perseus, had been invited to a great feast and had to bring extravagant gifts for the king. But

Perseus had nothing to give. Polydectes jeered at him.

"Look at Prince Perseus! See all his riches! The stench of fish and a wooden sword are his royal possessions!" As the guests laughed, Perseus flushed. To cover his embarrassment, he shouted,

**"I will return with a gift better than anyone else's."**

**"Impossible!" cried the king. "Only one treasure could be better than these."**

**"Name it!" challenged Perseus.**

**"The head of Medusa the Gorgon."**

**A hush fell.**

Perseus had heard of the three terrible Gorgon Sisters. From their backs sprouted eagles' wings. Their bodies were covered in iron scales and their hands were gnarled claws. From their faces grew ivory tusks. The two elder sisters had always been like this. Medusa, the youngest, had once been beautiful, with flowing black curls but was often very cruel. To punish her for a wicked deed, the gods had turned her hair into squirming, venomous serpents. All who looked on Medusa were immediately turned to stone.

"Until you return," gloated Polydectes, "your mother will remain my prisoner."

Perseus turned and strode out of the great hall.

# *GIFTS FROM THE GODS*

Perseus looked sadly out to sea. He had no weapons and no idea where to find the Gorgons. Worse still, his mother was in danger because of his foolish boast.

Then he saw two figures walking towards him; a tall woman wearing a gold helmet and carrying a shining shield, and a young man wearing winged sandals and carrying a curved sword.

He knew they must be Athena, the goddess of wisdom, and Hermes, the messenger god.

"Your father Zeus has sent us to help you," they told him. Perseus stood up in relief. Athena stepped forward.

"Take my shield," said the goddess. "Use it to look at the reflection of Medusa. Remember, never stare into her face for you will be turned to stone."

"Take my sword," said Hermes. "Its sharp blade will cut through iron."

"How do I find Medusa?" asked Perseus.

"Ask the Three Grey Sisters who live in the Cavern of Endless Night," they answered, and as quickly as they had appeared, the gods vanished. Clutching their gifts, Perseus found new courage and began his quest.

# *THE GREY SISTERS*

**The Cavern of Endless Night was close to the peak of a high mountain. As Perseus climbed, jagged rocks tore at his fingers and worn ledges crumbled under his feet.**

**At last, on a misty plateau, he found the Three Grey Sisters, so ancient that they had only one eye and one tooth, which they shared between them.**

The sisters were so busy cursing and bickering they ignored Perseus.

"Give me the eye!" demanded one.

"It is my turn. Give it to me!" said another, groping wildly.

"No it is still mine!" cried the last.

Perseus waited until the hag nearest to him held the eye. Jumping forward, he grabbed it, shouting, "I have your eye, now tell me how to find the Gorgons!"

The Grey Sisters screeched and snivelled, but they wanted their eye back.

"Go to the Garden of the Nymphs," one told him. "They can tell you."

"Where is the garden?" asked Perseus.

"At the back of the North Wind," the sisters wailed. "Now do give us our eye."

Perseus threw the eye into the lap of the first sister, hastily descended the mountain and turned north.

# *THE NYMPHS*

**At the back of the North Wind, Perseus found the beautiful Garden of the Nymphs. Golden fruits dropped from the trees. Rippling streams flowed over pebbles of precious gems. There, playing in the water, were the three Nymphs.**

**"We've been expecting you," called one Nymph. "The gods told us a brave hero will rid us of the Gorgon who threatens our beautiful land."**

**"Medusa's gaze turns gardens to desert," said another Nymph.**

**"And the desert creeps closer to us," said the third Nymph.**

**Then each gave Perseus a precious gift.**

**"These winged sandals," said the first, "will carry you swiftly through the air."**

"This magic sack," said the second, "will carry Medusa's head, so it cannot harm you."

"Wear this helmet," said the third, "and you will be invisible, so you can approach the Gorgons unseen."

Perseus thanked the Nymphs and asked how he might find Medusa. They told him of the Gorgons' barren island, not far away.

## *MEDUSA*

Wearing the winged sandals, Perseus flew to the island of the Gorgons. Deserts lay where gardens had been. Stone statues stood where once-living creatures had seen Medusa's face.

Looking into Athena's shield, Perseus saw the Gorgons sleeping. Even in reflection they were terrifying. Medusa's serpent hair twisted, hissed and spat.

Gathering all his courage, he put on his helmet of invisibility and flew down. His heartbeat was so loud that he was sure it would wake the sleeping sisters.

As he moved closer, the snakes hissed viciously and one of Medusa's eyes snapped open — and looked directly at him. Perseus froze, yet the hideous creature saw nothing.

**Perseus crept so close that he could feel the icy breath of Medusa. Raising the sword high above his head, he gave a mighty shout and with all his strength swung the blade. The severed head went flying and the snakes recoiled and spat. The shriek of the dying Gorgon echoed throughout the valley.**

**Perseus grabbed Medusa's head and thrust it into the magic sack. Using his winged sandals, he rose high in the sky.**

**As the two other Gorgons looked wildly around, a beautiful, winged, white horse rose from the headless corpse of Medusa.**

**Pegasus, the wondrous horse of the Olympian gods was born from the once-lovely Medusa, freed at last from the awful curse.**

# *ANDROMEDA*

As Perseus flew over the deserts the blood of Medusa seeped through the sack and dripped onto the ground below. Each drop created a lush, green oasis where it fell.

Reaching the seashore, Perseus saw a small figure. Swooping down he found a young woman chained to a rock.

"Who are you?" he asked. But the woman could see no one as Perseus was still wearing the magic helmet.

"Who is speaking?" she called.

As Perseus removed his helmet she saw with amazement a tall, handsome man carrying the weapons of a warrior.

"It is not safe here," she cried. "A ferocious sea monster terrorises these shores. You will be killed if you stay."

"What about you?" Perseus asked. "Who made you a prisoner here?"

"My name is Andromeda. My mother boasted about my beauty and made the Nymphs of the Sea jealous. They sent a monster to destroy my father's kingdom. The only way to stop the monster is to offer me as a sacrifice."

Perseus immediately cut the chain with his curved sword. Just then a great rumbling arose from the sea and a dragon reared its monstrous head.

Perseus drew
Medusa’s head
from the sack and thrust
it towards the creature’s face.
The monster’s roar was cut short as it
was turned to stone.

Perseus carried Andromeda back to her parents' home. Throughout the kingdom, there was a great celebration as the young man and woman were honoured for their courage.

Not long afterwards, Perseus and Andromeda happily announced that they wished to be married. After the wedding they left to return to Seriphos to free Danae from the clutches of the cruel Polydectes.

## *REVENGE*

In Seriphos, Perseus discovered that both his mother and Dictys, the fisherman, had been locked in prison.

Entering the great hall, Perseus stood again before the king.

"Here is Prince Perseus!" jeered Polydectes. "Where is the prize you promised?" Perseus raised the blood-stained sack with the head of Medusa.

"Behold your prize!" he said.

The king roared with laughter. He did not believe anyone could have slain the evil Gorgon.

Perseus lifted out Medusa's head and held it high for all to see. Suddenly the great hall became silent, as all who gazed upon the face of the Gorgon turned to stone. Polydectes' cruel reign was ended.

# *EPILOGUE*

King Acrisius heard of his grandson's great deed. Fearing Perseus would seek him out, Acrisius hid on the remote island of Larissa.

Athletic games were held annually on Larissa, and that year Perseus competed in the discus event. He threw the discus and watched in amazement as it flew far into the rows of spectators, striking an old beggar on the head. The beggar was killed instantly. He was Acrisius, who had hidden in the crowd to watch his grandson. And so the prophecy was fulfilled.

Perseus and Andromeda claimed Acrisius' kingdom, where they lived happily and ruled wisely.